This book
belongs to:

For my Dad

The Adventures of Camellia N.

The Arctic

Written by **Debra L. Widerøe**   Illustrated by **Daniela Frongia**

Notable Kids Publishing · Colorado
Printed in the USA

©2016 Debra L. Wiederøe
Written by Debra L. Wiederøe / Illustrated by Daniela Frongia
All words and illustrations ©2016 Debra L. Wiederøe.
All rights reserved. Published by Notable Kids Publishing, LLC
No part of this publication may be reproduced in any form without the written permission of the copyright owner or publisher.
For information contact Notable Kids Publishing, PO Box 2047 Parker, Colorado 80134
www.notablekidspublishing.com

Library of Congress Control Number: 2 0 1 6 9 0 0 8 0 5
Wiederøe, Debra L.
The Adventures of Camellia N. - The Arctic / Book 1 / written by Debra L. Wiederøe / illustrated by Daniela Frongia - 1st Edition
Summary: The Adventures of Camellia N. is the first in a series of nine educational fiction books targeted to children ages 4-8.
Camellia's nightly dreams take her on adventures to all seven continents and under the seas where she learns about and gains
appreciation for the environment surrounding her. The first book takes Camellia and her readers on an exciting journey to the Arctic.

ISBN 9780997085112
(Juvenile Fiction – ages 4-8)
Printed in the USA by Worzalla, Stevens Point, Wisconsin
Text fonts Black Magic & Helvetica
Illustrations were created using Cintiq and digitally airbrushed in Photoshop.

"Who is going with you on your adventure tonight, Camellia N.?"

her mother asked in a gentle voice.

"Puffy and Bear-Bear are coming with me.

I just can't wait! Good night, Momma. I love you so."

"Sweet dreams, little Camellia, Puffy and Bear-Bear.

Safe travels to you all."

Camellia yawned aloud, and closed her eyes as the moonlight lit up her room.

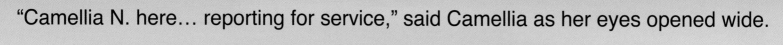

"Camellia N. here… reporting for service," said Camellia as her eyes opened wide.

Her lips were quivering from the bitter cold.

"Welcome to Icebreaker One. I'm Captain Lars and here is my crew,"

said the old man whose bushy beard glowed in the light.

"My team of scientists and I are here to explore the Arctic and show you our world.

But, before we begin our adventure, perhaps we should go inside the warm ship

and make you a nice cup of hot cocoa."

Camellia nodded, but quickly ran to the railing, screaming out with glee.

"Oh my, Captain Lars, my Bear-Bear has come to life!

There are bears dancing in the snow.

There are bears playing and others swimming in the sea,"

she said, pointing to the huge animals not too far from the ship.

"Yes. Those are our Arctic polar bears, the largest bears in the world,"

the Captain explained proudly.

Camellia was so excited she was almost out of breath.

"Well, I have never seen a real bear before and certainly not a polar bear.

I didn't even know they could swim."

"Perhaps one day your bear can come home with me, too.

I know he would like to play with Bear-Bear," she said thoughtfully.

"Although he might like a visit to your home, Camellia," said the Captain,

"Arctic polar bears need to stay right here in their home in the wild.

In fact, they need our sea ice to live."

"Well, I think they're just beautiful animals, so furry and bright

and white like the snow," Camillia stated. She then asked with concern,

"Captain Lars, are the bears very cold living here? Even though they are so big,

they don't have heavy parkas like we do to keep them warm."

"Oh, these bears are actually quite toasty warm, Camellia,"
the Captain replied tenderly. "Their fur, fat and even the snow they are
rolling around in keeps them very warm,
even during our freezing winters."

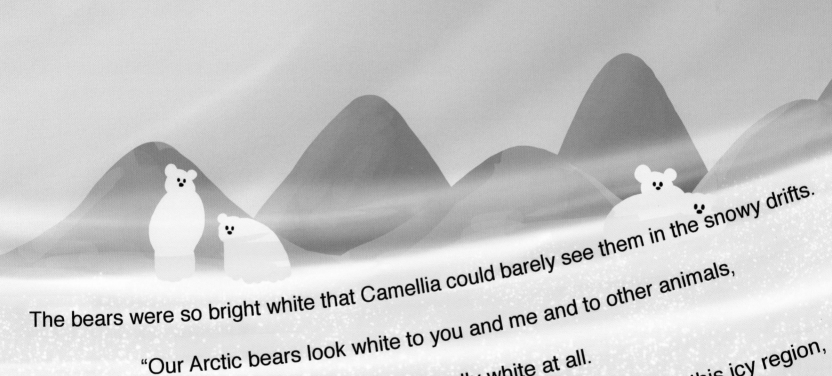

The bears were so bright white that Camellia could barely see them in the snowy drifts.

"Our Arctic bears look white to you and me and to other animals,

but they aren't really white at all.

Their hair serves as a disguise allowing them to hide very well in this icy region,

don't you think?" the Captain asked.

"They are beautiful animals and so very smart," Camellia said with delight.

"They dance, play, swim and even wear disguises. I just love the Arctic polar bears!"

Camellia watched the bears at play and hugged her Bear-Bear even tighter.

"There! Look over there in the water, Captain," Camellia shouted, her eyes sparkling bright.

"I hear a strange whistling sound and see a shiny white animal... or maybe it's a giant fish popping out of the water. Look! There he is and he's smiling at me."

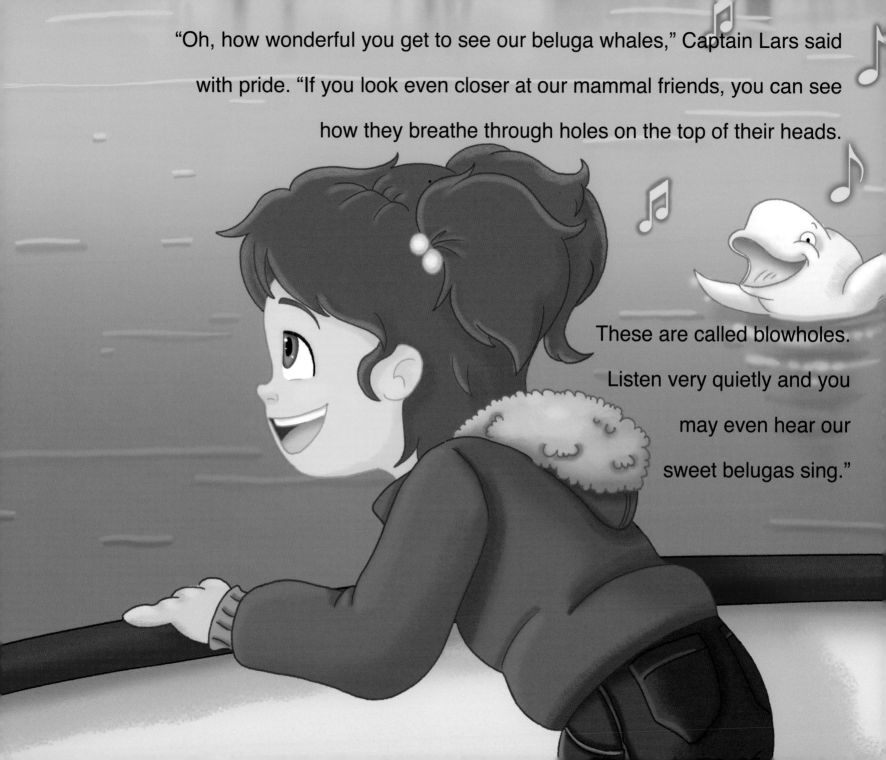

"Oh, how wonderful you get to see our beluga whales," Captain Lars said with pride. "If you look even closer at our mammal friends, you can see how they breathe through holes on the top of their heads.

These are called blowholes. Listen very quietly and you may even hear our sweet belugas sing."

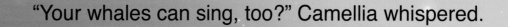

"Your whales can sing, too?" Camellia whispered.

"They're talking to me and making the funniest sounds I've ever heard."

"You are right, Camellia," said Captain Lars. "We call them sea canaries

because of these unusual sounds they make. And, since beluga

whales travel together in groups, called pods,

this is how they talk to each other."

"We need to take very good care of the belugas in the Arctic waters.

We want to make sure you see them for a very, very long time."

Camellia blew kisses to the belugas and waved goodbye.

"As we near the land, you may even see other animals hiding. Look closely, Camellia. We don't want to disturb them so we will be very careful to keep our ship at a distance."

"I think I do see an animal!"

Camellia squinted to see through the thick bed of snow.

"Yippee! I see the eyes of a very small animal, or maybe two or three.

I think they are all having fun playing hide-and-seek."

"What you see now is the Arctic fox," said the Captain. "It is one of our smaller Arctic friends, blending right in with the fresh snow. It is hard to see its body, isn't it?"

The Captain pointed to the animals as the ship got closer to the land.

"Not too far from our little fox is a herd of caribou, or what you might call reindeer."

"Of course I know what a reindeer is, Captain. Everyone knows that they have red noses and can fly," Camellia replied with a smirk on her face.

"Not these Arctic reindeer, little Camellia," he chuckled.

"Only Rudolph was lucky enough to have a red nose.

And, he also happens to be the only reindeer I know of that can fly.

But, these Arctic caribou are just as special too.

Not only do they have a keen sense of smell,

but they can see things that our eyes just can't see."

"Really, Captain?" Camellia said playfully.

"Can they see those silly white foxes hiding from us in the snow?"

"Well, yes they can, Camellia. Caribou have special vision.

The foxes actually look quite dark to a reindeer's eyes, like when we wear sunglasses.

Their unusual eyesight helps protect them from harm."

her green eyes sparkling like emeralds. "This is my most exciting adventure ever!"

"We're not quite done yet, Camellia. Look up into the sky!" the Captain shouted out.

"I can't believe my eyes.

It's green… and blue… and purple… and pink…

The sky is magical, too!

like ribbons dancing on a rainbow sky.

Why does your sky look like this, Captain Lars?"

"You're one lucky girl, Camellia N.," he said with delight.

"This is nature's most beautiful light show being performed just for you.

These magical lights are what we call the Northern Lights.

Isn't it simply amazing how the dancing colors light up our sky?"

Camellia stared at the colorful, lively lights as she yawned and rubbed her weary eyes.

"It's been a big day for you, little one," Captain Lars said sweetly.

"Let's go inside to warm up with that nice cup of hot cocoa I promised you earlier.

Just remember all of this beauty you see surrounding you, Camellia. It's all here for you."

Under a rainbow in the sky, belugas were singing their sweet melodies, bears gracefully skated across the ice, foxes were happily at play and caribou were dancing

"Thank you for the support. I am truly humbled." - Debbie

"The need to teach our children about stewardship of the environment has become increasingly more important. *The Adventures of Camellia N.* is a children's book series that not only educates young children with positive messaging, but helps propel them to action through Camellia Kids Care projects." I believe "we cannot accomplish all that we need to do without working together. Children are our future…and Camellia is an inspiring role model for them to become environmental ambassadors."

– Bill Richardson, The Richardson Center for Global Engagement; former two-term Governor of New Mexico, U.S. Congressman, U.S. Ambassador to the United Nations and former Energy Secretary of the United States

"The next 50 years will be critical in our effort to define the importance of wild spaces. History shows that people protect what they know and understand. By introducing young children to ambassador animals that depend upon endangered ecosystems for survival, Debbie Widerøe takes an essential first step. "The Adventures of Camellia N" provides parents and educators a creative and entertaining launch pad, from which they can introduce young minds to the magical beauty of the wild kingdom."

– Georgienne Bradley, Founder & Director, Sea Save Foundation

"Shooting a film on the human face of our shifting climate took me to the far corners of the world. The journey illuminated the spirit and dreams of young children globally. These young minds will inherit the problems we have allowed to manifest. Hybrid educational platforms like *The Adventures of Camellia N.* are a perfect vehicle allowing the dance between entertainment and education. There is no greater time to spawn a paradigm shift than a youthful and free mind."

– Michael P. Nash, Filmmaker

"Well done Camellia N! Books for children that are fun and also teach them about the wonders of nature are always so welcome. Caring about our shared planet can start before we learn to walk"

– Peter Boyd - Former COO of Carbon War Room & Founder of Time4Good

"*The Adventures of Camellia N.* inspires young readers to love and care for the Earth. Debbie Widerøe writes in a warm and lively style that will instantly captivate her readers. I truly love the series. Debbie has created a delightful gift to children."

– Esther Lindop, Author and Educator

To further explore the different parts of the world and "change the world together" please visit:

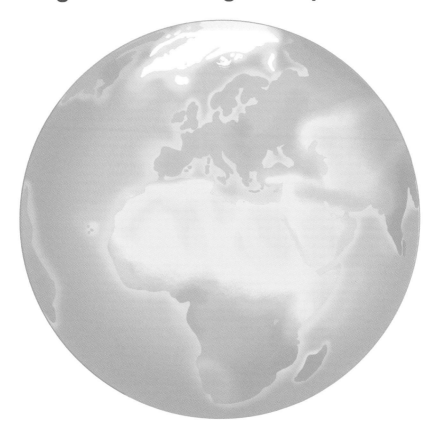

National Geographic Kids: kids.nationalgeographic.com
National Geographic: national.geographic.com